The idea of re-writing 'Thank You, Baked Potato' – which I originally sang on TV about twenty years ago – came to me on the 24th March 2020, when I was watching the news about the developing coronavirus situation. Despite the government's advice, people were still going out to pubs, restaurants and shops, so I wrote some new words to encourage them to stay in and also to help explain some vital new do's and don'ts to some of our younger friends. Two minutes later, I recorded it on my phone, uploaded it to Twitter and thought perhaps a couple of hundred people would see it. Within 48 hours it had been viewed three million times and I was recording it as a single (in my bedroom, of course), with all proceeds going to FeedNHS.

Thank you to Scott Coello for his wonderful illustrations, to Kevan Frost, who played all the instruments and produced the song, and to all of the amazing, kind people who have given their time for free to help me get the song (and now this book) to you. And lastly thank you to YOU for buying this book and supporting our heroic NHS workers.

Dedicated to the incredible NHS workers
and also to my housemate Jamie, who is isolating
with me and who has heard this song more times than
anyone should, and who has smiled throughout – M.L.

Dedicated to my husband John for enduring me always,
and Dora the dog (who can't read this) – S.C.

EGMONT
We bring stories to life

First published in Great Britain 2020 by Egmont UK Limited
2 Minster Court, London EC3R 7BB
www.egmont.co.uk

Text and illustrations copyright © Matt Lucas 2020
Illustrations by Scott Coello

Matt Lucas has asserted his moral rights.

ISBN 978 0 7555 0115 1

Printed in Great Britain

71438/002

A CIP catalogue record for this title is available from the British Library.

Egmont, Matt Lucas and Scott Coello are donating all profits from sales
of this book to FeedNHS, providing hot, nutritious meals for NHS staff
working in critical care in hospitals across the country.

www.thankyoubakedpotato.com
www.feednhs.com

THANK YOU, BAKED POTATO

MATT LUCAS

ILLUSTRATED BY
SCOTT COELLO

EGMONT

You must LISTEN

And if you want to have a BETTER DAY, you must LISTEN to what the BAKED POTATO say!

And if you want

to have a BETTER DAY . . .

the BAKED POTATO say!

2 METRES

B-A-K-E-D
P-O-T-A-T-O . . .
Baked Potato!

ENJOY YOURSELF INDOORS WITH THESE FUN ACTIVITIES!

MAKE A RAINSTICK

Tape up the end of a kitchen-roll tube, pour several handfuls of dried rice or lentils into the tube, then tape up the other end. Hey presto – a musical instrument that sounds like rain!

THEME DAY

Pick a favourite book, film or character and theme a whole day around it. Dress up, decorate your house, then come up with activities to fit. Fancy an Alice in Wonderland Day? Host a Mad Hatter's Tea Party! Make White Rabbit ears! Play pin the smile on the Cheshire Cat! And don't forget to stay in character . . .

MUSICAL STATUES

Dance till the music stops, then freeze and try your best not to move. For extra fun, give each round a theme: funny faces, monsters, elephants . . .

RECYCLED ART GALLERY

Use paint, stickers, glue and glitter to transform old containers into works of art. You could also use old keys, buttons, string, and even dried pasta. Find a place in your home to display your artwork then invite your family to come and admire it!

SCAVENGER HUNT

Ask an adult to make a list of things to search for in your home. The list could include objects, colours, patterns, material, letters, numbers . . . Check each object off the list when you find it!

THANKFUL JAR

Find an empty jam jar and decorate it using paints and stickers. Then cut a sheet of paper into strips and put them next to the jar. Every time you think of something you are thankful for, write it on a piece of paper and put it in the jar. Ask your family to do the same – and when the jar is full, get together with your family to read the messages!

COPYCAT DANCING

Pick a leader and copy their dance moves. Gradually add more moves till you have a dance routine to perform in front of your family!

WORD POOL POEMS

Cut up a sheet of paper into small pieces and write a word on each. Put them into a pile then pull out words to make a poem. Ask every member of the family to contribute to your word pool! You could also cut out words from newspapers and magazines.

EDIBLE ART

Find a space on the table then arrange fruit and veg to make a picture. Look carefully at the shapes, sizes and colours . . . Can you make a face? A flower? A house? A rainbow?

SOCK SKILLS

Use balled-up socks to practise your throwing and catching skills. Try throwing your sock-ball into a basket or box – moving it farther and farther away as your throws improve!

MATT LUCAS is an actor, writer and comedian, first coming to prominence in *Shooting Stars* with Vic Reeves and Bob Mortimer. Together with David Walliams, he reaped massive success with the smash-hit series *Little Britain*. The three BBC series and two Christmas specials won nearly every award for which they were nominated, including three BAFTAs, three NTAs and two International Emmy Awards.

Matt's film roles have included *Alice in Wonderland*, *Bridesmaids* and *Paddington*, as well as *Missing Link* and *Gnomeo and Juliet*. He has also appeared in a number of US comedy series, including *Community*, *Portlandia* and *Fresh Off the Boat*.

Back in the UK, Matt starred as series regular Nardole in *Doctor Who*, and fulfilled a lifetime ambition to appear in *Les Misérables*, playing Thénardier. He regularly presents shows on BBC Radio 2 and will soon be co-hosting *The Great British Bake Off*. His memoir, *Little Me*, was published in 2017.

SCOTT COELLO creates animations and illustrations under the alias Cribble. Cribble's humorous artwork and short films, from stories of human struggle to vignettes about dog farts, have been viewed by millions worldwide. *Thank You, Baked Potato* is Cribble's first picture book for children.